CORY THE CROCODILE

WRITTEN BY JOHN STORMS
ILLUSTRATED BY ROBERT STORMS

HEIAN

ISBN: 0-89346-530-5

Heian International
P.O. Box 1013
Union City, CA 94587

First printing 1993

97 96 95 94 93 10 9 8 7 6 5 6 3 2 1

Printed in Thailand

Hi! My name is Cory, and I'm a crocodile. I live in Africa--where you probably think all crocodiles live. Well, that's not true!

Crocodiles are found in places that have lots of water and hot weather--like South America, Asia, India, Australia, and Africa.

Do you know that we also live in the United States? As a matter of fact, my cousin Herman, the American crocodile, lives in Florida.

I love to visit him on my vacations!

Because we live next to rivers or lakes, can you guess
what our favorite pastime is?
It's swimming!

I like to spend the whole day in the water, swimming and diving and playing games with my friends. It's really fun to swim underwater and play hide-and-seek.

Now, you might think that, like a fish, I can breathe under the water. No way! I can hold my breath for a really long time, but I'm just like you--I have to come up for air. I'll bet that I can hold my breath longer than you can...at least, I <u>think</u> I can!

You know what else I can do? I can swim underwater with my eyes wide open! Even if I swim in a river that has really dirty water, I can still see. No, I don't wear a diving mask! That would look pretty silly, wouldn't it, with my **big**, **long** snout sticking out!

Actually, I have a pair of very special goggles that I wear all of the time. They're right under my eyelids, and I can see through them just like you can see through a window. They're great because they keep the water out of my eyes, and, best of all--I can't lose them! I'll bet you wish that you had goggles like mine!

Without special goggles like these, I might have to swim in dirty water with my eyes closed. Just think of what could happen then! I might bump into a rock or a log or maybe even a hippopotamus! And that could be very unhealthy for me!

Now that you know where I live, can you guess what my favorite food is? I'll give you a clue--it's not seaweed!

I LOVE FISH!!!!!

I could eat fish all day long...
just eat....
and eat...
and eat!
But, I do have one small problem.

I don't have a toothbrush!
And if you don't brush your teeth.....
what happens? First you get cavities....
OUCH!!!

Still later, your teeth might even fall out!
Can you imagine a toothless crocodile?
What a horrible thought!

But I'm lucky....
my best friend is a little bird named Bert,
and he helps me by being my own personal
toothbrush!

How does he do that, you might ask.
Well, after I eat one of my big fish meals
(and I <u>always</u> eat in the water), I usually have
lots of stuff stuck in between my teeth.

I crawl out of the water and then I'm ready for a nice long nap. I open my mouth in a great big yawn-- and my mouth stays open while I sleep!

While I'm sound asleep, Bert strolls into my mouth, just as brave as he can be!